DATE DUE

AUG 2 5 2009	JUN 3 0 2007	
AUG 2 7 2008	SEP 1 2 2008	
JUL 0 9 2004	AUG 1 2 2009	
JUL 3 0 2004	APR 0 6 2010	
DEC 0 7 2004	JUN 2 9 2010	
APR 0 8 2005	AUG 2 2 2011	
NOV 1 8 2005		
JUN 2 3 2006		
JUL 0 7 2006		
AUG 1 4 2006		
MAY 1 5 2007		

To Butch and Taylor

—JEA

Clarence and the Purple Horse Bounce into Town

by Jean Ekman Adams

rising moon

Clarence, Smoky, and their dog Edgar clop into the city. They have been Out West climbing mountains, crossing rivers, and camping out under the twinkly stars at night. Clarence can hardly wait to sleep in his own bed.

"We'll stay at my apartment with my sister Fern. She works in a string factory. Would you like to see her picture?"

"Not quite yet," says Smoky.

"Fern is a very good cook," says Clarence.

"I hope she has a lot of hay," replies Smoky.

Edgar hums excitedly.

They find Clarence's building on Eggplant Avenue, which has a big blue canopy,

a very small elevator,

and little round buzzers by all the doors.

"Fern!" squeaks Clarence. "This is my friend Smoky.
I brought him home from my vacation. He lived on a
ranch. And this is our dog Edgar, who hums and dances."

"Oooh, what a handsome
creature!" Fern kisses Edgar
on the nose and her nephew
Tiny falls out of her pocket.
Edgar jumps up and down
and says, "Hello!"

Hello?

Clarence and Smoky have
never heard Edgar speak.
They nearly fall over
with surprise.

Clarence notices Fern has redecorated the apartment.
His nose starts to twitch.

"Clarence tells me you like to eat plants," says Fern.

"Hay," corrects Smoky politely.

"I love to cook plants. Tonight I will make you my
famous spinach tasties!"

It is wonderful being back in the city. Clarence feels quite
bouncy. First, he takes Smoky shopping at a big department
store, where they pick out new horse pajamas.

Then they visit the park, where Clarence points
out the very sparkly sidewalks.

They take Edgar to the aquarium to visit Bubbles.
Edgar doesn't like being away from Fern.

"Guess what we're having for lunch today," says Fern.

"Hay?" asks Smoky hopefully.

"Wrong! Eggplant rollups!"

They lean out the window to look at the rooftops. Clarence's ears
flap in the wind. He notices that Smoky tries to look Out West.

One day, Clarence and
Smoky take a floating tour
of the harbor. Clarence
has too many sno cones.

When they get back home, Fern is knitting Edgar
a fluffy little vest out of leftover string.

"Guess what's for dinner!" she says.

"Hay?" guesses Smoky.

"Wrong! Avocado boats with smashed potatoes!"

They all sleep like rocks.

Clarence wants to show Smoky a fancy restaurant with big napkins and lots of silver forks. They get all dressed up and go out to eat.

"I have already ordered," says Fern importantly. "Carrot blobs for everyone!"

After dinner, Clarence asks, "Edgar, do you notice that Smoky is not looking well? A little pale, perhaps?"

Edgar hums happily and says, "Hello!"

Clarence sighs and presses on his nose. And he worries.

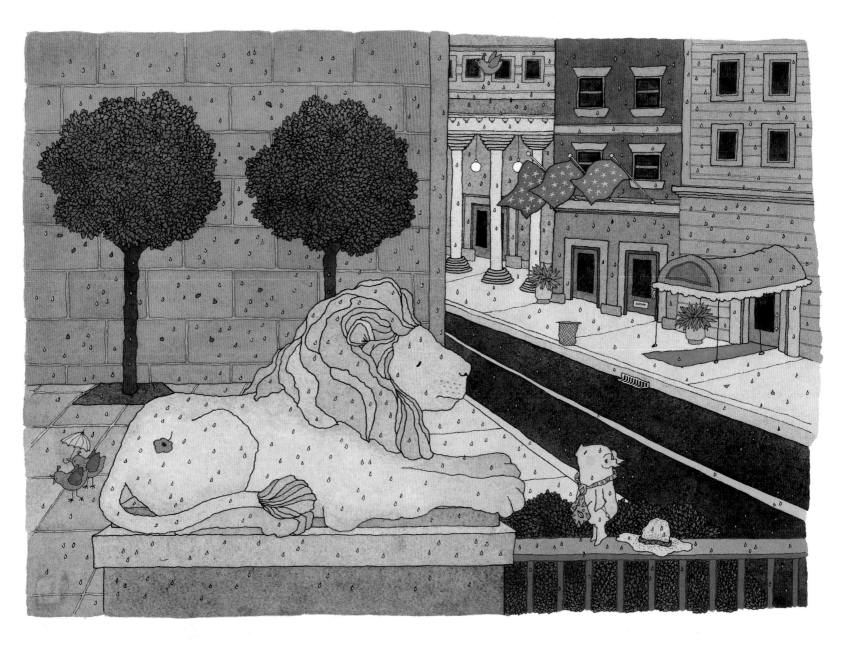

The next day, Clarence was going to take Smoky to the library to
see the lions. He goes by himself. He does not have a good time.

When Clarence gets home, he sees the duck doctor from upstairs inspecting Smoky. The doctor listens to Smoky's stomach and peeks down into his ears.

"What have you been feeding this horse?" he quacks.

"Only the best," answers Fern. "Spinach tasties, eggplant rollups, avocado boats, smashed potatoes, and carrot blobs. Edgar loves my cooking."

The doctor sighs and says, "This horse is fading fast. He needs clean mountain air and plain grass hay."

Clarence nearly stops breathing. Smoky fading? Mountain air? Grass hay? What is he talking about?

"Where can I find that in the city?" he squeaks.

"You can't," says the doctor. "This horse must be bundled up and sent back Out West. And soon!"

Smoky packs sadly. He doesn't have a lot to pack.

"I will miss you, little Clarence," he says, patting
Clarence carefully with his hoof.

Before Clarence knows it, Smoky is gone.

What to do, what to do, what to do,
agonizes Clarence, pressing on his nose.
Let Smoky go? By himself? Or go with
him? But leave the city? So soon? Leave
the apartment and his bed? Leave the
sparkly sidewalks and the sno cones?
Leave Fern's cooking? And Edgar?

Clarence thinks of Smoky on the bus all alone.
Maybe he won't know how to work the reclining
seats. Maybe he won't know where to get off
the bus. Maybe he will get bus-sick.

Clarence can only think of one thing to do.

Pack, pack, pack.

Hug, hug, hug.

Run, run, run!

"Wait, wait, wait!" squeals Clarence.

Smoky is amazed to see Clarence on the bus.

"Fern is cooking broccoli bombs for dinner tonight and Edgar wanted to stay. They will visit us on their vacation."

"What??" says Smoky.

Clarence climbs up into the bus seat. He is nearly out of breath. "I decided I better come with you," he explains. "You might have trouble with your pajamas or something."

Smoky opens his eyes wide. Really wide.
And then he turns purple.

Really, really, really purple.

Jean Ekman Adams grew up watching her father, illustrator Stan Ekman, paint in his studio at home. It never occurred to her that she would follow in his footsteps, but she has been an artist for thirty years, exhibiting in galleries across the country. Today she is pursuing her career as an author and illustrator of children's books.

Jean's son Taylor thought up the concept of Clarence and Smoky, based on their family dentist named Clarence, who owned a horse named Smoky. Smoky is a real rescued horse, who lives in peaceful retirement in Tucson, Arizona. Although he is not purple, Smoky is a loyal, honest, and faithful creature—just like his namesake in the book.

Jean lives in Arizona with her husband and son, where she often rescues animals. She currently has two pugs, three cats, a determined mule, and a very sweet burro. In the summers they all escape to Colorado, where the Clarence books were largely written and illustrated.

Other Rising Moon books by Jean Ekman Adams:

Clarence Goes Out West and Meets a Purple Horse
Clarence and the Great Surprise

www.northlandpub.com

Composed in the United States of America
Printed in Hong Kong

Edited by Theresa Howell
Designed by David Jenney
Production supervised by Donna Boyd

FIRST IMPRESSION 2003
ISBN 0-87358-826-6

03   04   05   06   07   5   4   3   2   1

Library of Congress Cataloging-in-Publication Data

Adams, Jean Ekman, 1942-
Clarence and the purple horse bounce into town / written and illustrated by Jean Ekman Adams.
p. cm.
Summary: Clarence the pig is excited about coming back to the city after being out
West, but when the food and air do not suit his friend Smoky the purple horse, they both
decide to leave.
[1. City and town life—Fiction. 2. Friendship—Fiction. 3. Pigs—Fiction. 4.
Horses—Fiction. 5. Food habits—Fiction.] I. Title.

PZ7.A2163 Cn 2003
[E]—dc21   2002073966